THE LITTLE HORSE BUS

Also in this series:

The Little Train
The Little Fire Engine
The Little Steamroller

THE LITTLE HORSE BUS
by Graham Greene

Illustrated by Edward Ardizzone

RED FOX

THE LITTLE HORSE BUS
A RED FOX BOOK 978 1 782 95283 1

First published in Great Britain by The Bodley Head,
an imprint of Random House Children's Publishers UK
A Penguin Random House Company

The Bodley Head edition published 1974
This new format Red Fox edition published 2015

1 3 5 7 9 10 8 6 4 2

Text copyright © 1952 Verdant SA
Illustrations copyright © Edward Ardizzone, 1973

The right of Graham Greene and Edward Ardizzone to be identified as the author and illustrator of this work
has been asserted in accordance with the Copyright, Designs and Patents Act 1988.

Red Fox Books are published by Random House Children's Publishers UK,
61–63 Uxbridge Road, London W5 5SA

www.**randomhousechildrens**.co.uk
www.**randomhouse**.co.uk

Addresses for companies within The Random House Group Limited can be found at: www.randomhouse.co.uk/offices.htm

THE RANDOM HOUSE GROUP Limited Reg. No. 954009

A CIP catalogue record for this book is available from the British Library.

Printed in China

Penguin Random House is committed to a sustainable future for our business, our readers and our planet.
This book is made from Forest Stewardship Council® certified paper.

Everybody for miles around Goose Lane used to buy their groceries at Mr Potter's Shop. He had three assistants and Tim

the errand boy and three cats
to keep away mice. He also had
a pony called Brandy. He had
bought Brandy from a man
who was cruel to him and he

kept him in the yard to play
with the children. His
customers told him all their
troubles and sometimes

he would slip a bag of lollipops into a basket and say, "With the compliments of the firm, madam." (That was when a child was ill.)

But one sad day when Mr Potter came back from a holiday at the seaside he found a big new grocer's shop just across the street. It was a horrible shop with a horrible name. Turn over and you will see it.

It was called the Hygienic (which only means clean) Emporium (which only means shop) Company Limited (and that means it was owned by Sir William Popkins, who never came into the shop and never put lollipops in bags.

He thought lollipops were cough-drops and you bought them at a chemist's. Sir William Popkins is too ugly to draw.)

The children all stayed with Mr Potter, but they only had pennies to spend, which hardly paid for Brandy's sugar.

Mr Potter could no longer afford the three assistants.

First he had two, then he had one, and then he only had Tim.

Tim sniffed a lot. He was not hygienic.

At last even the cats had to go.

The Hygienic Emporium delivered the parcels in a hansom cab with a smart chestnut mare called Beauty. The driver wore a top hat and he carried a whip with ribbons.

It was a very smart turn-out and pleased the grown-ups. They felt rather grand when the hansom stopped at their doors. But the children didn't like Beauty. She was too proud to eat sugar.

Mr Potter had only Tim.

Mr Potter closed the shop and went home to his little flat in Goose Lane Mews. He had only taken two shillings and

sixpence three farthings. He thought, "It's the end." The rain came down and the wind blew, and when Mr Potter tried to cook a kipper for his supper the gas went out because he hadn't paid the gas bill. Mr Potter went hungry to bed.

He couldn't sleep. "If only I had a hansom cab," he thought, "Brandy could draw it and Tim could drive it, and I would have an extra nosebag in which I could put the lollipops." But what was the good of dreaming? "I am ruined completely," Mr Potter said, "but I wish that door in the yard wouldn't bang so." He put on his boots and went downstairs. A garage door banged and banged: nobody had mended the lock. Inside Mr Potter saw many strange objects, shrouded and knobbly, with queer corners.

Mr Potter barked his shin on something round with spokes. "Oh dear, oh dear, what will people leave lying around next?" He lifted up a tarpaulin and shone his flashlight, and this is what he saw. There were spiders' webs everywhere and empty bottles and tins and broken china and a chair with only three legs – and dusty and neglected in the corner the little horse bus.

Mr Potter had an idea. Brandy should pull the little horse bus!
Next day he put a notice in his shop window. "All my customers
will come back to me," he thought, but the
hansom cab only
laughed proudly.
He wouldn't even
speak to the

horse bus when they met on their rounds,
for Mr Potter could not afford any paint
and polish and Brandy was very thin

(you can't live on lump sugar) and
Tim – well, Tim was still Tim.

"He's not hygienic," the customers said and only one old lady who had driven in a horse bus years ago when she was a girl returned to Mr Potter's shop.

Mr Potter didn't know what to do next. He couldn't afford Tim any more. He had a sad talk with Tim. Tim wiped his nose and sniffed. Mr Potter increased his wages.

Then he had a sad look at Brandy. He felt Brandy's ribs and gave him four more lumps of sugar. He walked all round the horse bus and wiped it softly with the corner of his apron. It was very dusty.

Every Saturday morning the hansom cab took the money people had paid for their groceries to the bank: sacks of copper pennies and sacks of silver shillings and a bag full of pound notes. The bank manager received the hansom cab very respectfully at the door.

Little did they know who was watching them.

Puzzle: find the thieves.

The thieves are wanted by the police.

They are two very bad men. Mr Potter saw their pictures outside the police station when he went to work.

One Saturday morning the little horse bus was trailing wearily through the streets. Oh how tired he was. He had nearly lost his self-respect, and when a bus loses his self-respect it is time to be broken up and turned into wooden boxes and tintacks and all the things an old bus is turned into.

At the corner of Chancery Lane, a policeman held him up.

Suddenly – BANG, CRASH, RUMBLE, RUMBLE, RUMBLE – right past the policeman with a high squeak and a crack, crack, crack went . . . Was it? No. The little horse bus couldn't believe his eyes. It was the hansom cab, but who was that on the box? "Thieves," Brandy whinnied, and "After them," cried the little horse bus, creaking in all his axles. They started off so quickly that Tim fell off the driver's seat, and they went on alone.

The traffic policeman, when he saw the thieves drive past, called the police station on the telephone, and the police station called Scotland Yard where the important detectives are. "Calling all cars, calling all cars," went the wireless.

But the cars got mixed up in Piccadilly Circus and only one pursuer remained on the trail of the stolen hansom cab; Thunder – thunder – crack – crack – crack went the hansom cab, and creak – creak – grind – grind – grind – oh-my-old-wheels went the little horse bus.

"Drat that silly old bus," said the thieves. "Can we never be rid of him?"

They dropped bottles to cut poor Brandy's feet.

And everyone came out of The Red Cow to watch the chase.

The little bus creaked and Brandy panted.

But the hansom cab was still in sight. Suddenly the traffic lights changed and it was lost in a cloud of dust.

The thieves beat poor Beauty till she squealed.

"Who would think an old horse bus could keep up so long?" they said. They were clever men and they knew just where they were going. When they had shaken off all pursuit they had a hiding place prepared, a dark dreary yard on the banks of the Thames. There they would shut poor Beauty in ("and let her starve to death," they said, "for all we care") while they escaped in a boat with all the stolen money. This was how they had planned it.

"We've lost them," said Brandy. "We might as well go home. I am hungry." But then the little horse bus felt his heart ache for the hansom cab in the hands of those cruel men.

He knew too well what it felt like to be abandoned. "We go on till we drop to pieces," he said to Brandy. All through the night he trailed, up one street and down another, looking for a clue.

Meanwhile the police looked for clues too. They took finger prints off the red pillar box.

No two people in the world have the same finger print. Put a little ink on your thumb and press it on a piece of paper.

You will see that nobody could mistake your finger print for the thieves'.

But though they had found the finger prints the police hadn't found the thieves.

"Let's go home," Brandy implored. "We've done all we can." But what was that dark shiny thing lying in the gutter?

"The lamp of the hansom cab," exclaimed the little horse bus. "Don't you see? It was knocked off when they passed that lamp there."

They stared and stared at the grim doors in that dark, dreary yard. It was marked HANGMAN'S WHARF.

"We'd better go and find a policeman," said Brandy.

"No time. No time," said the little horse bus. "Back six paces and then – CHARGE!"

There was an important ceremony the next day. Sir William Popkins was there, looking sheepish, and all of Mr Potter's old customers.

"I congratulate you," said the Commissioner of Police to Mr Potter, "on having such a brave little horse bus, and I have been asked to hand you this cheque for a thousand pounds."

Bravo

Hurray

Hear hear

Mr Potter was too excited to say anything, but he looked at the little horse bus with tears in his eyes.

Nobody thought any more about the Hygienic Emporium. It had to close down for want of customers. Everybody wanted to see the brave little horse bus, so they all came to shop at Mr Potter's.

"What is the good of dreaming?" Mr Potter had wondered, but turn the page and you will see that sometimes dreams come true.